She

Make friends with

Sheltie™

The little pony with the big heart

Sheltie is the lovable little Shetland pony with a big personality. His best friend and owner is Emma, and together they have lots of exciting adventures.

Share Sheltie and Emma's adventures in

SHELTIE THE SHETLAND PONY
SHELTIE SAVES THE DAY
SHELTIE AND THE RUNAWAY
SHELTIE FINDS A FRIEND
SHELTIE TO THE RESCUE
SHELTIE IN DANGER
SHELTIE RIDES TO WIN
SHELTIE AND THE SADDLE MYSTERY
SHELTIE LEADS THE WAY
SHELTIE THE HERO
SHELTIE IN TROUBLE
SHELTIE AND THE STRAY
SHELTIE AND THE SNOW PONY
SHELTIE ON PARADE
SHELTIE FOR EVER
SHELTIE ON PATROL

Peter Clover was born and went to school in London. He was a storyboard artist and illustrator before he began to put words to his pictures. He enjoys painting, travelling, cooking and keeping fit, and lives on the coast in Somerset.

Also by Peter Clover in Puffin

The Sheltie series

Sheltie
and the Foal

Peter Clover

PUFFIN BOOKS

For Jan Payne

PUFFIN BOOKS

Published by the Penguin Group
Penguin Books Ltd, 27 Wrights Lane, London W8 5TZ, England
Penguin Putnam Inc., 375 Hudson Street, New York, New York 10014, USA
Penguin Books Australia Ltd, Ringwood, Victoria, Australia
Penguin Books Canada Ltd, 10 Alcorn Avenue, Toronto, Ontario, Canada M4V 3B2
Penguin Books (NZ) Ltd, Private Bag 102902, NSMC, Auckland, New Zealand

On the World Wide Web at: www.penguin.com

Penguin Books Ltd, Registered Offices: Harmondsworth, Middlesex, England

First published 2000
2

Sheltie is a trademark owned by Working Partners Ltd
Copyright © Working Partners Ltd, 2000
All rights reserved

Created by Working Partners Ltd, London W6 OQT

The moral right of the author has been asserted

Set in 14/23 Palatino

Made and printed in England by Clays Ltd, St Ives plc

British Library Cataloguing in Publication Data
A CIP catalogue record for this book is available from the British Library

ISBN 0-141-30803-6

Chapter One

It was a sunny Saturday morning in
Little Applewood. Emma leaped out
of bed and padded barefoot across
the floor to her bedroom window.

She flung open the curtains and
smiled as she saw Sheltie, her little
Shetland pony, waiting patiently by
the paddock gate. As soon as he saw
Emma, Sheltie flung up his head and

said 'good morning' in his special pony way, by calling to her with a noisy snort.

Emma got dressed and hurried downstairs. Outside, the sky was the brightest blue, with fluffy clouds

chasing each other across the distant hills.

'Breakfast!' called Emma as she raced down the garden path and swung her legs over the paddock fence.

Sheltie was being extra cheeky this morning. He nudged Emma playfully on the bottom as she landed. This knocked her off balance and made her sit down with a bump. Emma was now the right height for Sheltie to nuzzle through the top of her hair with his soft nose.

'Get off!' said Emma, giggling. She pushed Sheltie away gently and jumped to her feet. Then she flung her arms around the Shetland pony's neck and gave him a big hug and a kiss.

Sheltie blew a raspberry and pushed his head into Emma's arms for another hug. While she was giving him his cuddle, Emma thought of Tracy Diamond and her pony, Blaze. Tracy was one of Emma's friends from school.

'I hope Blaze is OK,' said Emma. Sheltie pricked up his ears and listened to Emma's voice as he followed her to the field shelter for his breakfast. 'Blaze is going to have a foal. Tracy's really excited, but she's a bit worried about Blaze, in case something goes wrong.'

Emma scooped pony mix into

Sheltie's feed manger, and stroked his neck as the Shetland lowered his head to eat.

'The foal is due any day now, Sheltie. Shall we go for a ride over to Redroofs and see if there's any news?'

Sheltie threw back his head and blew a ripple through his lips. He still had a pony nut in his mouth and he sent it whistling over Emma's head.

'Does that mean you like the idea?' said Emma, laughing.

Sheltie opened his big brown eyes wide. He always liked going out for rides with Emma, no matter where they went.

'Then that's what we'll do this morning, Sheltie. I'll have *my* breakfast, then I'll phone Sally and see if she wants to come with us for a ride over to Redroofs.'

Emma walked back up the garden

path to the cottage, leaving Sheltie
snuffling around in his bedding
straw in search of his stray pony nut.

Tracy Diamond lived on the far side
of Little Applewood, behind Barrow
Hill. She lived in a white
stonewashed house called Redroofs.
It was a big house, surrounded by
trees, with a paddock just like
Sheltie's.

Emma met up with Sally and
Minnow at the little stone bridge just
outside the village.

'Hello, you two,' she called as she
trotted up on Sheltie.

Minnow was drinking from the
stream as they approached. He was a

black and white piebald. He was also Sheltie's best pony pal.

'Hi, Emma. Hello, Sheltie,' answered Sally. She greeted her friend with a big grin.

When Sheltie saw Minnow drinking, he decided that *he* was thirsty too. He sank his muzzle below the cool water and blew lots of bubbles. He wasn't really drinking at all though. As usual, Sheltie was being playful.

Minnow finished and licked his lips. Then he nibbled Sheltie's ears and the two ponies rubbed noses.

'Sheltie never changes, does he?' said Sally, laughing. 'He's always playing the clown!'

Emma smiled. Sally thought
Sheltie was great too. Emma was
glad that she had her as her best
friend.

The two girls rode their ponies down the country lanes. Then they crossed open fields until they could see red roof-tiles peeping through the trees in a hollow behind Barrow Hill.

Emma was very excited. 'Blaze might have had her foal already,' she said. 'I can't wait to see it!'

Chapter Two

Emma and Sally ambled up the drive
to Tracy's house on their ponies.
Sheltie kept snatching at the bushy
green hedges that overhung the
gravel path. Minnow was very well-
behaved and walked in a perfect
straight line.

'Sometimes,' said Emma to Sheltie,
'I wish that you were as good as

Minnow. But most of the time I love you just as you are – naughty and mischievous.'

Apart from the soft clip-clopping of the ponies' hoofs and the creak of leather saddles, all was silent.

'It's very quiet,' whispered Sally.

'Almost too quiet,' said Emma. She began to feel a bit concerned.

The sudden trill of a bird from a nearby tree broke the eerie silence as they reached the top of the drive.

'Look!' exclaimed Emma. 'That's Mr Thorne's car.'

Mr Thorne was the vet. His green Land Rover was parked right outside Blaze's stable.

At that moment, Mr Thorne ran

out from the stable to fetch
something from his car. His white
shirtsleeves were rolled up and he
looked very worried.

He saw the two girls and called
out to them before he dashed back to
the stable. 'It's not a good time for a
visit just now,' he said. 'I think it
might be best if you went home.' The
vet smiled and tried to sound
friendly, but his face was set with
concern.

'I wonder what's happened,' said
Sally. She turned Minnow easily and
waited for Emma to get Sheltie to
turn round.

'It's got to be Blaze. She must be
having her foal,' said Emma as she

struggled with Sheltie. 'Come on, boy,' she pleaded. But Sheltie seemed determined to carry straight on, right into the stable.

Finally, Emma managed to face him towards home. But Sheltie

wasn't happy at all. He snorted and complained and kept looking behind him as they walked slowly back down the drive, away from the house.

'I hope everything's all right,' said Sally anxiously when they finally stood side by side out in the lane.

'I've got a horrible feeling it's not,' said Emma glumly. 'Sheltie was acting really strangely. He seemed determined to get into the stable to see Blaze. He's not normally *that* naughty when I ask him to do something.'

'Mr Thorne looked worried too, didn't he?' said Sally.

'And if *he*'s worried,' exclaimed

Emma, 'then something is definitely *very* wrong.'

They sat on their ponies for a moment, in silence.

'We could phone!' Emma cried out suddenly. Her voice startled Minnow, who skipped sideways and nearly stumbled into a ditch.

'Oops! Sorry,' said Emma.

Sally was a brilliant rider and quickly calmed Minnow down. 'I wish he wouldn't do that,' she said.

'It was my fault,' admitted Emma. 'I shouldn't have called out like that.'

'But you're always yelling,' teased Sally. 'He should be used to you by now! Now what *exactly* were you trying to say?'

Emma grinned. She liked it when Sally teased *her* for a change.

'We could phone,' said Emma. 'Then we could ask Tracy if Blaze is OK.'

'Do you think that's a good idea?' asked Sally. 'Maybe we should wait until tomorrow or until we see her at school on Monday. If something *is* wrong, then Tracy will probably be really upset. She may not want to talk to anyone today.'

'But we might be able to do something to help,' insisted Emma.

'Mr Thorne did ask us to go away,' Sally reminded her.

'But he didn't say anything about not telephoning,' said Emma.

'No, but I really think we should wait until tomorrow and phone then,' replied Sally firmly.

Emma realized that Sally was probably right. Tomorrow just seemed like such a long way away. And Emma really wanted to know what the matter was *now*!

Emma and Sally spent the rest of the morning riding, thinking up names for Blaze's foal and hoping that everything was all right with both mother and baby.

At lunchtime, Sally had to go home. She was going shopping with her mum that afternoon.

'New school shoes,' moaned Sally.

'Yuk!' Emma pulled a face. 'Come

over early tomorrow. We'll phone Tracy together, first thing!'

The two girls said goodbye, then rode off in opposite directions. But when Emma and Sheltie arrived home, Mum was waiting at the paddock gate with some really terrible news.

Chapter Three

'I've just spoken to Mr Thorne on the telephone,' said Mum. 'I'm afraid I've got something really sad to tell you.'

Emma gripped Sheltie's reins tightly.

'Mr Thorne thought you would want to know that Tracy's pony has had her foal –' Mum went on.

'We guessed that,' said Emma,
without waiting for Mum to finish.
'That's brilliant news.'

'Well no, I'm afraid it's not so
good,' said Mum. She placed her
hand on Emma's arm and continued.

'Blaze was very sick and there were complications, Emma. Tracy's poor pony died giving birth to her baby.'

'Oh, no!' Emma let go of Sheltie's reins and her hands shot up to her mouth. 'Blaze is dead? It can't be true!'

'I'm afraid it is,' said Mum sadly. 'The vet thought you should know in case you had any plans to go visiting again. It's best if you stay away for a few days, Emma. Tracy's very upset.'

Emma tried to imagine how Tracy must be feeling. She felt really sick herself just thinking about it. Emma leaned forward across Sheltie's neck and gave him a huge hug.

'Poor Tracy,' she said. Emma could

feel tears stinging her eyes. 'And poor, poor Blaze.' She thought for a while, then sat up in the saddle. 'What will happen to the foal?' she asked. 'Will it be able to live without its mother?'

Sheltie flicked back his ears. Although he couldn't understand what Emma and her mum were saying, he was listening to their voices. And somehow he seemed to know that something was wrong.

'The foal has to be bottle-fed by hand and looked after twenty-four hours a day,' said Mum. 'Mrs Diamond doesn't know much about ponies, so Mr Thorne has asked Marjorie Wallace to help. She's had lots of experience with sick and orphaned animals.'

'I could help too,' piped up Emma. 'I could go over to Redroofs, and Sally would want to come and help as well, I'm certain of it.'

Mum raised her eyebrows and squeezed Emma's shoulder.

'Unfortunately, there's a problem there,' said Mum. 'Tracy is very upset at losing Blaze. She's blaming the foal for taking Blaze away from her. In fact, she's so upset, she doesn't want to keep him.'

'Oh, but that's awful!' cried Emma. 'She can't mean it. The baby foal needs looking after just as much as poor Blaze did. Tracy can't possibly mean it! She loved Blaze.' Fresh tears of sadness welled up in Emma's eyes.

Sheltie twisted his head round and tried to nuzzle Emma's foot in the stirrup. The little pony could tell that she was upset.

'If I went and talked to Tracy,

25

maybe I could persuade her to change her mind,' suggested Emma.

'That's a very nice thought,' comforted Mum. 'But Tracy needs time to get over Blaze. And the baby needs help *now*.'

Emma knew that Marjorie was kind and very good with animals. The old woman would do everything she could for the foal.

'Perhaps I can help Marjorie,' said Emma. 'When will she start looking after the foal?'

'Mr Thorne has already taken him over to her cottage,' said Mum. 'Maybe you can go and see Marjorie tomorrow. But it might be best to let her settle Star in first.'

'Star,' said Emma. 'What a beautiful name.'

'The vet named him,' said Mum. 'Apparently he's got a white mark on his forehead in the shape of a star.'

Emma couldn't wait until tomorrow. She wanted to ride over straight away to see if there was anything she could do to help. She finally persuaded Mum to let her go. But first, Mum went inside to telephone Marjorie and make sure that it would be OK.

'Now promise me that you won't get in Marjorie's way,' said Mum as she came outside again. 'And don't stay too long!'

'I promise,' said Emma. 'I'll just

see if there's anything I can do to
help.'

Sheltie pricked up his ears and
blew a soft snort. He seemed to be
telling Emma that he wanted to help
too!

Emma decided to call in for Sally
on the way. She spent the ride to Fox

Hall Manor thinking about poor Tracy and Blaze.

Emma was sorry that Blaze had died, but she really wanted Tracy to forgive and accept Star. After all, it wasn't the baby foal's fault. Somehow, with Sheltie's help, Emma was going to try to patch things up.

Chapter Four

When Emma broke the news to her friend, Sally could hardly believe it.

'That's awful,' said Sally.

The two friends gave each other a hug.

'Can you imagine how it would feel if anything like that happened to Sheltie or Minnow?' said Sally.

Emma remembered how she had

felt when Sheltie had broken his leg.
It was horrible – the worst feeling
ever. But Sheltie had got better,
unlike Blaze.

'Let's just hope there's something
we can do to help,' Emma said.

Sheltie interrupted by poking his
nose in-between the two girls. He

wanted a hug too. Sally and Emma
made a big fuss of the little pony.
Then they did the same to Minnow
so that he wouldn't feel left out.

Minutes later they were out in the
lane, on their way to Marjorie's cottage.

Marjorie Wallace lived with her
brother Todd in a cottage at the foot
of Beacon Hill. They had a big
rambling garden, and fields with a
fenced-off paddock.

Marjorie was always looking after
animals. She collected strays and
found homes for them.

'The last time Sheltie and I went to
Marjorie's cottage,' said Emma, 'she
had *eleven* cats.'

Sheltie tossed his head and sent his long mane flying out to the side as they trotted along.

'Sheltie knows where we're going, don't you, boy?' said Emma.

The little pony sniffed the air and blew a snort.

'See?' said Emma, laughing. 'He just said "Yes".'

'I know ponies aren't supposed to understand us,' said Sally, grinning, 'but sometimes I really think that Sheltie knows exactly what you're saying.'

'Of course he does,' joked Emma.

Sheltie snorted again and set Minnow off.

'Now he's telling Minnow,' Emma

said with a laugh.

'If I didn't know better,' said Sally, 'I could *almost* believe you!'

Up ahead sat Beacon Hill, like a huge upturned pudding basin. Marjorie's cottage was on the far side. It was built on the grassy slope, at the foot of the hill, where the beacon flattened out to fields and meadows.

The first part of the cottage they saw was the tall stone chimney pot.

'There it is!' cried Emma. 'Not far now. I can hardly wait to see Star, can you?'

Sally nodded. 'I want to see him, but I can't stop thinking about Tracy.'

'I know,' said Emma. 'Poor Tracy

needs as much help as Star. And I think the best way to help both of them is to get them back together.'

Sheltie leaned over Marjorie's front-garden gate and slid the bolt across, using his lips.

'I still don't know how you taught him to do that,' said Sally in amazement.

'I didn't,' said Emma, grinning. 'Sheltie taught himself.'

They rode the two ponies up to the front door and dismounted. Normally, Emma would have ridden Sheltie straight round to the back, but she didn't want to surprise Marjorie, in case she was busy with the foal.

Instead, Emma and Sally tethered Sheltie and Minnow to the big metal ring in the wall and politely rang the doorbell.

It seemed to take ages before anyone answered it. But suddenly Sheltie pricked up his ears and Emma knew that someone was coming.

The door swung open and Todd stood there looking tired and very worried. He smiled when he saw the girls and went over to ruffle Sheltie's forelock.

'How's Star?' asked Emma straight away.

Todd shook his head from side to side. 'Not very good, I'm afraid.

We've been trying to get him to take
a bottle. But the little fellow doesn't
want to know. We've managed to
give him enough milk to keep him
alive, but what he really needs is a
good feed.'

'Will it be all right for us to see him?' asked Emma. 'Maybe we could try to feed him! I've fed lambs with a bottle on Mr Brown's farm.'

'I'm sure Marji will be happy for you to try,' said Todd. 'If you can get the little one to take the bottle, you'll be doing everyone a big favour.'

They went inside the cottage and headed for the kitchen door, which led out to the back. Emma looked round to see Sheltie straining on his reins and peering after them through the open door. The Shetland pony didn't like Emma going off without him. He sniffed deeply and blew a soft whicker.

Marjorie was outside in the small

barn. She was sitting on a bale of hay
with her arms around the little foal,
giving it affection and warmth. A
baby's bottle filled with milk lay on
the bed of straw near her feet.

'Hello, you two. Come in,'
whispered Marjorie, putting a finger
to her lips.

At first, Star looked like he was
sleeping peacefully, but as soon as he
noticed Emma and Sally, he became
instantly alert. He struggled away
from Marjorie on skittish, unsteady
legs and tried to hide at the back of
the barn.

'It's all right, baby,' soothed
Marjorie. 'Come on. It's all right.
They're your friends.' She held her

arms open and gently coaxed the foal back to her.

Emma and Sally couldn't take their eyes off Star. The little foal was so beautiful. He was a light rusty-brown colour – a strawberry roan like his mother – with a white star-shaped mark on his forehead. His legs were longer than Emma could possibly have imagined. And his eyes were big and round with curious wonder as he gazed at the two girls.

'Look at his funny little mane,' whispered Emma. 'It's all short and tufty like a brush.'

'He's *so* sweet,' said Sally. 'I've never seen anything so lovely.'

But Star was trembling from head
to tail. His long, thin legs were
shaking so much that he could
hardly stand.

Marjorie stroked his furry face and tried to soothe him with her soft voice.

'Come over and say hello,' she whispered to Emma and Sally. 'But speak nice and quietly – no sudden movements. The poor little thing is very confused and frightened at the moment.'

Chapter Five

Emma and Sally edged their way
forward as quietly as they could. The
foal watched their every move as
they shuffled through the straw.

'Hello, little Star,' whispered
Emma softly.

Sally held out her hand for the foal
to sniff. But Star was nervous and
timid, and shied away.

'Don't be scared,' said Emma. She moved further forward and continued speaking, slowly and softly. Star's nostrils twitched.

'He can smell pony on you,' smiled Marjorie. 'It's a familiar smell for him, so he trusts you and knows you won't harm him.'

Star seemed to relax and finally Emma was able to touch his soft, woolly coat. She spoke gently to the foal while she stroked his neck and face, and he sniffed at her clothes.

'Why don't you try him with the bottle?' suggested Sally. 'Maybe you could get him to drink something.'

'It would be wonderful if you could,' said Marjorie. 'This is special

milk from the vet. So far we've only
managed to get a tiny bit of it down
him. He *must* start feeding properly
soon or he'll be too weak to survive.'

Emma carefully took the bottle and held it towards Star's mouth. The little foal sniffed at it, but pulled away.

'Come on, Star,' whispered Emma. 'Please drink some, even if it's just a tiny mouthful.'

But Star didn't want to know.

Sally began to stroke the little foal too. 'You've got to feed or you won't grow big and strong like your ...'

Emma guessed she was about to say 'mother', but had suddenly remembered that Star didn't have a mum any more.

'You've got to feed, because you've got to grow big and strong to help Tracy,' finished Sally.

All of a sudden, there was a very loud neighing coming from the front of the cottage. Star's ears pricked up straight away at this new sound. He cocked his head to one side, alert and listening.

'That's Minnow!' exclaimed Sally. 'I wonder why he's making that dreadful noise!'

'Sheltie's probably teasing him,' suggested Emma. 'I'd better go and take a look.' She slipped quietly out of the barn and went round the side of the cottage. But as she turned the corner she saw Sheltie cheekily clip-clopping straight through the front doorway. Emma guessed that Sheltie had been straining so hard on his reins, trying to see where she had gone, that he'd slipped his tether.

She hurried through the cottage after the Shetland pony and caught up with him in the doorway of the barn.

Sally and Marjorie couldn't believe their eyes when they saw Sheltie coming into the barn – and neither could Star.

The little foal stared at the Shetland pony with eyes the size of saucers. Then he made a funny whimpering noise through his lips.

At first, Emma thought that Star might be scared of Sheltie. But he wasn't. Sheltie blew a very soft snort

and the little foal bounded towards
him on his long rubbery legs.

Sheltie and Star rubbed noses.
Then the little Shetland pony licked
Star's forehead and washed his ears.

The foal closed his eyes and nuzzled up close to Sheltie's warm flanks.

Star leant his head against Sheltie's side and nibbled at the Shetland pony's thick coat with his soft lips.

'I bet Star thinks that Sheltie is his mother,' said Sally.

This suddenly gave Emma an idea.

She called to Sheltie in a hushed whisper. 'Here, Sheltie. Here, boy.'

Sheltie came over straight away. And little Star followed. He was still trying to nuzzle up as close as he could to the Shetland pony.

Emma ruffled Sheltie's long mane and gave him a pat. Then she took the feed bottle, loosened Sheltie's girth, and slipped the bottle underneath the leather strap.

Sheltie looked back at the feed bottle and blew a soft whicker.

This time the little foal needed no encouragement. He found the bottle immediately and took the teat in his mouth.

Emma, Sally and Marjorie held

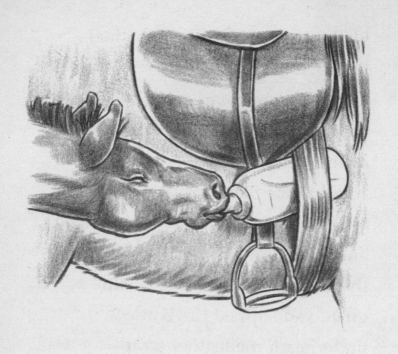

their breath and watched in silence as Star drank the milk.

'This is fantastic,' whispered Marjorie. '*We* couldn't get him to feed properly, but he's taking it from Sheltie. What a good idea, Emma!'

Emma and Sally just couldn't stop

looking at the two little ponies.
Emma was so pleased that she had
been able to help, even though it was
really Sheltie who had started Star
feeding with the bottle.

When Star had drunk half the milk
Marjorie unstrapped the bottle from
Sheltie. This time, she tried holding
it out for the foal. But Star wouldn't
take it from her. He would only
drink freely from the bottle if it was
slipped through Sheltie's girth strap.

'Oh dear,' said Marjorie anxiously.
'If that's the only way he's going to
feed, then we've still got a big
problem!'

Chapter Six

'Star needs to be fed regularly, with special milk from the vet, every two hours,' explained Marjorie. 'It's very important that he continues feeding if he's going to survive.'

Emma looked at Sally. She had a good idea what the old woman was going to say next.

'How would you feel about letting

Sheltie stay here for a while?'
Marjorie asked. 'You can come and
visit him as often as you like, after
school and at the weekends. And you
know that we would take very good
care of him, don't you? He could
stay in the paddock with his donkey
friends, Mudlark and Sophie.'

Suddenly, Emma had lots of
butterflies fluttering in her tummy.
She wanted to help the baby foal, but
she really didn't like the idea of
leaving Sheltie behind. Emma wasn't
sure what to say.

'It might not be for too long,' said
Marjorie. 'We may get Star to bottle-
feed by hand in a day or two. But it
could take quite a lot longer.'

Emma looked at Sally, then back at Star, who was feeding hungrily from Sheltie's bottle.

Emma realized that there was only one answer to Marjorie's question.

'Of course Sheltie can stay,' she said. It was the only way that Star would survive. And if Emma was going to reunite Tracy with Blaze's foal, then she had to make sure that little Star was healthy and strong.

Emma turned to Sheltie. 'I want you to stay here for a while and help Star,' she said to the pony. 'It won't be for long, boy.'

She gave Sheltie a big hug and said goodbye. The little Shetland pony whickered gently and pushed his face against Emma's. She couldn't help it when her eyes filled with tears. Sally had to give Emma a hug and tell her not to be silly.

'I promise you, we won't give up trying,' said Marjorie. 'As soon as

Star takes the bottle by hand it will be easy for us to feed him regularly and Sheltie can come home to you.'

'I'll bring you over on Minnow every day after school, Emma,' offered Sally. 'And we can come at the weekend. The time will go by really quickly, you'll see.' She gave Emma's arm a squeeze.

'Goodbye, boy,' said Emma, giving Sheltie another big hug. 'Be good. I'll come and see you every day. I promise. You *do* understand why I'm leaving you here, don't you, Sheltie?'

The little Shetland tossed his head back, then poked out his tongue and blew a cheeky raspberry.

'There's no doubt about it now!' said Sally, laughing. 'I'm absolutely certain that Sheltie understands everything you say!'

Sally went to fetch Minnow. She rode him round to the back, then held her hand out and gave Emma a lift up behind her. Emma made herself comfortable on Minnow's rump. She gave Sheltie a final wave as they rode away, and stopped herself from looking back, but there was a big lump in her throat.

'It won't be for long,' said Sally reassuringly. 'Sheltie will be back home in his paddock really soon.'

'I know,' said Emma with a sniff. 'But I miss him already.'

They rode all the way back to Emma's cottage in silence.

'It was a really nice thing to do,' said Mum, 'and very thoughtful. Well done.' She knew that Emma was trying to be brave and was already missing Sheltie enormously. 'He'll be perfectly all right,' Mum went on. 'Marjorie's an expert with animals, especially ponies. And just think, Sheltie's helping to save that little foal's life.'

'I know,' said Emma, feeling a bit brighter. 'And while Sheltie is helping Star, I'm going to help Tracy. I'm planning to have a talk with her at school on Monday.'

*

But when Monday came, Tracy
didn't feel like talking to Emma. She
was still very upset, and the last
thing she wanted to hear about was
baby Star. It seemed that all Tracy
could think about was Blaze.

After school, Emma walked back
with Sally to her house. They
changed out of their school uniforms
and pulled on jeans and sweatshirts.
Emma had taken hers to school in a
bag along with Sheltie's pony rug.
Then the two girls mounted Minnow,
and Emma hung on to Sally as the
piebald pony trotted smoothly along
to Beacon Hill.

When they arrived at Marjorie's

cottage Sheltie was so excited he
galloped around the paddock,
kicking up his heels, with little Star
following close behind.

The first thing Emma did was give
Sheltie a big hug. Then she brushed

the forelock out of his eyes and
palmed him a peppermint treat.

'I've brought your pony rug and
I've got a carrot for you to have
later,' whispered Emma.

But Sheltie wanted his carrot *now*.
He could smell it in Emma's jeans
pocket, and wouldn't stop nibbling
and nudging her until she gave it to
him.

'You never change, do you?' said
Emma, grinning.

'He's been making us laugh all
day, haven't you, Sheltie?' said
Marjorie as she walked out of the
barn.

'How's Star?' asked Emma. She
could see that he was following

Sheltie around everywhere. 'Is he letting you feed him by hand yet?'

Marjorie shook her head. 'I'm afraid not. He still only feeds from Sheltie. But he's getting stronger by the hour.'

It was true. Emma could tell that Star was much steadier on his legs and his eyes were bright and alert.

She stretched out her hand, and the foal left Sheltie's side to come over for a friendly sniff. He seemed to remember Emma and closed his eyes as she gently stroked his face and neck.

She tried again to tempt Star with the bottle, but the little foal turned his head away.

Emma was pleased that Sheltie was able to help. She was secretly hoping that Star would be feeding by hand very soon though, so that Sheltie could come home.

But it was the same the next day and the day after. Star would still only drink milk from Sheltie's bottle.

On Thursday, when Emma and Sally saw Star for the sixth time, Sheltie had been away from home for five whole days.

'What if Star *never* takes the bottle from anyone except Sheltie?' said Emma anxiously.

The two girls were watching the little foal gambol around the paddock on his long, rubbery legs with Sheltie, Mudlark and Sophie.

Sheltie came up to the paddock fence, and Emma stroked him through the rails.

'Star does look really strong now,' said Sally. 'I'm sure that Marjorie will soon be able to feed him herself, by hand.'

'I hope so,' said Emma. She was really missing Sheltie now. Not having him at home was proving to be very hard. 'I don't think I can bear leaving Sheltie here for much longer,' she added. 'I miss him too much.'

Chapter Seven

The next day at school, Emma
decided to talk to Tracy Diamond
again. She had thought of a clever
plan to reunite Tracy and Star – and
to get Sheltie home. The first thing
she had to do was to persuade Tracy
to come to Marjorie's cottage to meet
Star.

This time, Tracy seemed ready to

talk about the little foal. Emma told her about how Sheltie was helping him, and Tracy listened carefully to every word.

'At first, I couldn't understand why you didn't like little Star,' said Emma. 'I knew you were *really* upset about losing Blaze, but I still thought it wasn't fair to blame Star. That's why I wanted to help – and now I've ended up losing Sheltie.'

'You haven't lost Sheltie,' said Tracy. 'He'll probably be back home with you in a day or two.'

'No, he won't,' argued Emma. 'I know he's not gone for ever, but I still feel like I've lost him.' Emma was trying really hard to make Tracy understand. 'If Blaze's foal doesn't take the bottle, it could be months and months before I have Sheltie home again.'

'Do you think it could be that long?' asked Tracy.

'I *know* it will be,' said Emma with a sigh. 'Now I understand why you hate the little foal.'

'Oh, I don't hate him,' said Tracy. She sounded rather surprised that Emma should think she did.

'But you don't *like* him, do you?' continued Emma.

'Well, it's not that I don't *like* him,' began Tracy.

'You probably would like Star if you saw him,' said Emma. 'He *makes*

you like him. He's all fluffy and wobbles about on these really long legs like Bambi. And when he looks at you with his big brown eyes, it makes your heart melt!'

'It sounds as if *you* really like him,' said Tracy.

'I did at first,' said Emma. 'But now I'm starting to hate him!'

'You can't mean that!' gasped Tracy. 'You and Sheltie are helping to keep him alive.'

'I know,' said Emma. 'But how can I like him when he's taken Sheltie away from me?'

'Star hasn't done it on purpose though,' explained Tracy. 'He's probably confused and frightened. And he just thinks of Sheltie as his best friend.'

'But Sheltie's *mine*,' said Emma sadly. 'He's *my* best friend. Not Star's!'

'It must be rotten,' said Tracy. She felt really sorry for Emma now. 'I wish I could do something to help.'

'Well, maybe you can,' said Emma.

'What?' asked Tracy. 'What can *I* do?'

'You can come and see Star,' said Emma. 'And you could try him with a bottle. You never know, he might take it from you.'

'Why should he take it from me and no one else?' asked Tracy.

'Don't know,' said Emma, shrugging casually. 'But it's worth a try!' So far, her plan was working perfectly. 'Why don't you come and meet Sally and me at Marjorie's tomorrow?' she said. 'You might be able to help me get Sheltie back.'

'I could ride over on my bike,' offered Tracy.

'OK.' Emma smiled. 'We'll see you there at ten.'

At ten o'clock the next day, Emma and Sally were waiting at Marjorie's cottage for Tracy to arrive. Emma was chatting to Marjorie and explaining part two of her plan.

'Well, anything is worth a try,' said Marjorie. 'Star still hasn't taken the bottle from anyone except Sheltie, and he's due for a feed now.'

'Let's wait for Tracy,' said Emma. 'I've a funny feeling my plan's going to work.'

Sheltie was in the paddock with
Mudlark, Sophie and the little foal.
They were having a game of chase.
Star was chasing both donkeys
round in big circles. His long,

rubbery legs bucked and bounded as he struggled to keep up.

Tracy pulled up on her bike and smiled as she watched the game.

'Hi, Tracy.' Emma called her friend over to the paddock. 'He's beautiful, isn't he?' she said.

'Yes – and he's grown,' said Tracy. 'He was really tiny when I first saw him.'

'Look at those legs,' said Emma, smiling. 'Any minute now, they're going to tie themselves up in knots.'

'They *are* long,' said Tracy, laughing.

Star was trotting around the paddock, kicking up his heels.

'I'm amazed he doesn't hurt

himself,' said Sally. 'He's leaping around like a young deer.'

'I didn't realize he was so cute,' said Tracy.

'Let's go into the paddock and see if we can get him to come over.' Emma called out to Sheltie. She knew that Sheltie would come running across straight away. And that meant baby Star would come too.

'Why don't you wrap Sheltie's pony rug around you?' said Emma. The rug was draped over the paddock fence. Emma picked it up and handed it to Tracy.

Tracy looked puzzled.

'Star doesn't know you,' explained

Emma, 'but if you wore Sheltie's rug, he might catch Sheltie's scent and be more friendly.'

Tracy did as Emma suggested. Suddenly she *wanted* the little foal to be friendly. She wanted to see baby Star close up.

Emma, Sally and Tracy crouched down as Sheltie came trotting over with Star close at his heels.

Emma made a big fuss of Sheltie and deliberately ignored Star. But the little foal wanted some fussing too. So when Tracy reached out, Star was happy to be petted. Suddenly, the foal caught the scent of the pony rug and pushed his head right into Tracy's arms for a closer sniff.

Star looked up at Tracy with his big melting eyes and made a funny snuffling snort. And Tracy burst into tears.

Chapter Eight

Marjorie placed a comforting arm around Tracy's shoulders as Star pushed his head into the folds of the pony rug.

'He can smell Sheltie,' whispered Marjorie kindly. She pressed the feed bottle into Tracy's hand. 'Would you like to try him with this?' she asked. 'It's very important that Star feeds by hand,' she added.

Tracy wiped away her tears and took the bottle. Both Emma and Sally held their breath as Tracy offered the feed to Star.

The little foal blinked his long lashes and looked up at Tracy adoringly. Then he glanced at the bottle and turned his head towards Sheltie.

Sheltie blew a soft snort, and nudged Star gently towards Tracy.

For a moment, Star hesitated. He sniffed at the teat of the bottle. Tracy held it steady.

'Please,' whispered Emma. 'Please take it, Star.'

The little foal pushed at the teat

with his soft velvet muzzle. Then he whickered and began to drink the milk.

'Yes!' Emma wanted to jump up and shout really loudly. But she didn't. She knew she couldn't.

Sally nudged her gently in the ribs and pressed a finger to her lips. 'Shhh!'

'I know,' whispered Emma. 'But the plan worked! It's brilliant, isn't it?'

Everyone stood very still and quiet as Star drained the bottle. When he had finished, the rubber teat plopped out of the foal's mouth with a 'pop'. Then he burped.

This made Tracy giggle. She really

wanted to look after the little foal now. 'It wasn't your fault that I lost Blaze,' she said to Star, giving him a cuddle. 'You lost your mother too. That must have been awful for you, you poor little thing.'

The baby foal nuzzled into Sheltie's rug and closed his eyes.

'Do you think you might be able to try again later with another bottle?' asked Marjorie.

'I'd really like that,' said Tracy.

Emma winked at Sheltie and his bright eyes sparkled beneath his bushy forelock.

'It looks like Sheltie might be going home any time now,' said Sally.

Emma put her arm around Tracy. 'If Star is lucky, he'll be going home too,' she said.

Tracy smiled. 'If I didn't know you better, Emma Matthews, I'd say you planned the whole thing.'

'You don't mind, do you?' confessed Emma. 'Only I had to think of a way to get you here. I knew once you saw Star you'd want to take him home. And I made up the bit about starting to dislike him. Sorry! But it *did* work, didn't it? It got you here! And it was really *you* that got him to feed!'

'I don't mind at all,' said Tracy. 'I was being selfish and stupid, I suppose. You and Sheltie made me realize that Star needs me. He's an orphan now, and he needs a family to care for him.'

'So you think you might want to take him back?' asked Marjorie. 'I'll happily look after him until you make your mind up properly.'

'Thanks.' Tracy smiled. 'I've already made up my mind though. He'll never replace Blaze, but he's Blaze's baby, and I know she would have wanted me to look after him. I can't wait to tell my parents. They've been trying to get me to come and see Star all week, just like Emma.'

'And no one's more pleased that you came than baby Star,' said Marjorie.

*

That afternoon, Star was taken back to Redroofs and Sheltie went home with Emma.

'It's all turned out brilliantly,' Emma told Mum. 'Tracy's going to look after Star, and I've got Sheltie back!' She felt so happy that she flung her arms around the little pony and gave him a special hug.

Sheltie closed his eyes and gave a soft snort. He seemed glad to be home too.

At Redroofs, Tracy and her mum and dad were making arrangements for Star's welfare. He was still very young and really needed some company.

'We're going to look for an old
rescue pony to keep Star company,'
Tracy told Emma and Sally when
they visited the next day. 'I don't

want another riding pony just yet,'
she added. 'And a quiet old pony in
need of a safe, warm stable will be a
comfort for Star.'

'What a great idea,' said Emma.

'It will be fantastic to watch Star
grow up,' said Sally. 'I bet he turns
into a brilliant pony.'

'Just like his mother,' said Emma.

'And just like Sheltie,' said Tracy,
smiling. She ruffled the Shetland
pony's scruffy mane and laughed
as he blew her a loud raspberry.
'Star wouldn't be here if it wasn't
for Sheltie,' she said. 'He's the
best!'

Emma grinned. She knew that
Tracy really meant it. And it made

her feel so proud. She felt she was the luckiest girl in the world to have a pony like Sheltie.

If you like making friends, fun, excitement
and adventure, then you'll love

The little pony with the big heart!

Sheltie is the lovable little Shetland pony with a big
personality. He is cheeky, full of fun and has a heart
of gold. His owner, Emma, knew that she and Sheltie
would be best friends as soon as she saw him. She
could tell that he thought so too by the way his
brown eyes twinkled beneath his big, bushy mane.
When Emma, her mum and dad and little brother,
Joshua, first moved to Little Applewood, she thought
that she might not like living there. But life is
never dull with Sheltie around. He is full of
mischief and he and Emma have lots of exciting
adventures together.

Share Sheltie and Emma's adventures in:

SHELTIE THE SHETLAND PONY
SHELTIE SAVES THE DAY
SHELTIE AND THE RUNAWAY
SHELTIE FINDS A FRIEND
SHELTIE TO THE RESCUE
SHELTIE IN DANGER

READ MORE IN PUFFIN

For children of all ages, Puffin represents quality and variety – the very best in publishing today around the world.

For complete information about books available from Puffin – and Penguin – and how to order them, contact us at the appropriate address below. Please note that for copyright reasons the selection of books varies from country to country.

On the World Wide Web: www.penguin.co.uk

In the United Kingdom: Please write to *Dept. EP, Penguin Books Ltd, Bath Road, Harmondsworth, West Drayton, Middlesex UB7 0DA*

In the United States: Please write to *Penguin Putnam inc., P.O. Box 12289, Dept B, Newark, New Jersey 07101-5289* or call 1-800-788-6262

In Canada: Please write to *Penguin Books Canada Ltd, 10 Alcorn Avenue, Suite 300, Toronto, Ontario M4V 3B2*

In Australia: Please write to *Penguin Books Australia Ltd, P.O. Box 257, Ringwood, Victoria 3134*

In New Zealand: Please write to *Penguin Books (NZ) Ltd, Private Bag 102902, North Shore Mail Centre, Auckland 10*

In India: Please write to *Penguin Books India Pvt Ltd, 11 Panscheel Shopping Centre, Panscheel Park, New Delhi 110 017*

In the Netherlands: Please write to *Penguin Books Netherlands bv, Postbus 3507, NL-1001 AH Amsterdam*

In Germany: Please write to *Penguin Books Deutschland GmbH, Metzlerstrasse 26, 60594 Frankfurt am Main*

In Spain: Please write to *Penguin Books S. A., Bravo Murillo 19, 1° B, 28015 Madrid*

In Italy: Please write to *Penguin Italia s.r.l., Via Felice Casati 20, I-20124 Milano*

In France: Please write to *Penguin France S. A., 17 rue Lejeune, F-31000 Toulouse*